Favorite Fairy Tales

Three Little Pigs

Retold by Rochelle Larkin   **Illustrated by Loretta Lustig**

CREATIVE CHILD PRESS
is a registered trademark of Playmore Inc.,
Publishers and Waldman Publishing Corp., New York, N.Y.

Once upon a time, there were three little pigs who lived with their mother. One day, she decided that the little pigs were big enough to make their own way in the world.

So off they went, each in a different direction,
to seek their fortunes.

The first little pig was walking along the road when he met a man with a wagon full of straw. Well, thought the pig, I can use the straw to build myself a house. So he took the straw, and settled in.

One day, as he was sitting inside, a big bad wolf came by.
"Little pig, little pig, let me come in!" he howled.
"Not by the hair of my chinny chin chin," cried the little pig.
"Then I'll huff and I'll puff and I'll blow your house in!" said the wolf.

Then the wolf huffed and he puffed and he puffed and he huffed. The straw house fell right down, and the little pig ran away to find his brothers.

The second little pig met a man with a pile of sticks. He used the sticks to build himself a house. It was just finished when the first little pig came running up.

"The big bad wolf blew down my house of straw," he cried.
"My house is made of sticks," the second little pig said proudly.
"The big bad wolf can't blow that down."

The two little pigs were just sitting down to lunch when the wolf came to the house of sticks.

"Little pigs, little pigs, let me come in!" he howled at them.

"Not by the hair of our chinny chin chins!" called back
the little pigs.

"Then I'll huff and I'll puff and I'll blow your house in!" said the wolf. He huffed and he puffed and he puffed and he huffed, and down came the house of sticks.

The two little pigs had just enough time to run away to find their brother.

The third little pig met a man with a load of bricks. Just the thing to build a good strong house with, thought the pig.

He built his house smoothly and carefully and just in time to greet his two brothers.

The three little pigs went inside. The third little pig hung a big kettle of water to boil in the fireplace to make soup for their dinner.

Soon enough, along came the big bad wolf.
"Little pigs, little pigs, let me come in!" he howled.

"Not by the hair of our chinny chin chins!" said all the little pigs together.

"Then I'll huff and I'll puff and I'll blow your house in!" threatened the wolf.

Then he huffed and he puffed and he puffed and he huffed and he huffed and he puffed again, but all his huffing and all his puffing couldn't blow down the house of bricks.

The big bad wolf was very angry. He sat down to think what else he could do to get to the little pigs. Then he had an idea.

The big bad wolf sneaked around the brick house.
Then he climbed up on the roof.
Slowly, he started to climb down into the chimney.

As he looked down the chimney, he saw the big kettle of boiling water the pigs had set out to make their dinner. Back up to the roof he scrambled as fast as he could.

The wolf jumped up on the roof and then down from the house. He ran away as far and as fast as he could.

The three little pigs watched happily as the wolf ran out of sight.

Then they sat down to their dinner and never were bothered by the big bad wolf again.